"THEY MAY LAUGH AT MY FLAWS, BUT..."

THURD/WIRM MEDIA EUGENICS PRESENTS

"THEY MAY LAUGH AT MY FLAWS, BUT..."

By
Fault Dizzney

A hilarious book of reminders on God's loving promises to imperfect souls that you'll read so fast, it'll make your head grin...

iUniverse, Inc.
Bloomington

"THEY MAY LAUGH AT MY FLAWS, BUT..."

iUniverse books may be ordered through booksellers or by contacting:

iUniverse
1663 Liberty Drive
Bloomington, IN 47403
www.iuniverse.com
1-800-Authors (1-800-288-4677)

ISBN: 978-1-4697-6461-0 (sc)
ISBN: 978-1-4697-6462-7 (e)

Printed in the United States of America

iUniverse rev. date: 06/05/2012

WHEREVER WOULD GOD'S PEOPLE BE WITHOUT THE KINDNESS OF *STRANGLERS...*

Hi folks! If you're like me, joke-writer Fault Dizzney, you've at some point probably felt pretty insecure because of your looks, qualities, stations in life or unflattering comments people have made that choke the confidence out of you.

Good news! The Bible is God's series of love letters to us stating how crazy He is about you and me – no matter the world's glamour standards. Check out a few of the, uh, "constructive" things people have said about me...and a few wonderful things Christ loves to re-emphasize concerning me (and YOU)...

I'VE HEARD IT SAID ABOUT ME THAT...

"Yeah, he survived a bout with cancer. But his skull has always been so pointy that after chemotherapy and losing his hair, he had to wear a motor-oil funnel."

BUT GOD'S LOVE LETTERS ARE A REMINDER TO ME THAT...

I will praise thee; for I am fearfully and wonderfully made: marvelous *are* thy works; and *that* my soul knoweth right well.

-- Psalm 139:14

I'VE HEARD IT SAID ABOUT ME THAT...

"Those gigantic horse teeth of his are so discolored that when he yawns, people think he's wearing a brown blindfold."

BUT GOD'S LOVE LETTERS ARE A REMINDER TO ME TO PONDER FIRST, THEN REMEMBER...

What is man, that thou art mindful of him? and the son of man, that thou visitest him? For thou hast made him a little lower than the angels, and hast crowned him with glory and honour.

-- Psalm 8: 4, 5

I'VE HEARD IT SAID ABOUT ME THAT...

"He's so hideously unattractive that when his mother saw her sonogram, she strung up a noose and tried to hang herself by the waist."

BUT GOD'S LOVE LETTERS ARE A REMINDER TO ME THAT...

Herein is love, not that we loved God, but that he loved us, and sent his Son *to be* the propitiation for our sins.

-- 1 John 4:10

I'VE HEARD IT SAID ABOUT ME THAT...

"That porker is so fat that when he walks, even his feet jiggle."

BUT GOD'S LOVE LETTERS ARE A REMINDER TO ME THAT...

I say unto you, that likewise joy shall be in heaven over one sinner that repenteth, more than over ninety and nine just persons, which need no repentance.

-- Luke 15:7

I'VE HEARD IT SAID ABOUT ME THAT...

"The stuff he owns is so old that every month, his suits receive a social-security check."

BUT GOD'S LOVE LETTERS ARE A REMINDER TO ME THAT...

Before I formed thee in the belly I knew thee;

-- Jeremiah 1:5

I'VE HEARD IT SAID ABOUT ME THAT...

"His elephant-sized eyeglasses from the Helen Keller collection get a big thumbs-up. That poor sap's vision is so bad that last night, he couldn't untie his shoe laces until they finished bathing his guide-dog."

BUT GOD'S LOVE LETTERS ARE A REMINDER TO ME THAT...

Thou hast beset me behind and before; and laid thine hand upon me.

-- Psalm 139:5

I'VE HEARD IT SAID ABOUT ME THAT...

"Seriously, he must gargle with sewer-sludge. His breath is so bad, his reflection hides in his shadow."

BUT GOD'S LOVE LETTERS ARE A REMINDER TO ME THAT...

For whatsoever is born of God overcometh the world: and this is the victory that overcometh the world, *even* our faith.

-- 1 John 5:4

I'VE HEARD IT SAID ABOUT ME THAT...

"His jaws are so flabby that every time he sneezes, he slaps the people ahead of him."

BUT GOD'S LOVE LETTERS ARE A REMINDER TO ME THAT...

By this I know that thou favourest me, because mine enemy doth not triumph over me.

-- Psalm 41:11

I'VE HEARD IT SAID ABOUT ME THAT...

"The guy is so tight with money that every year, he makes his children pay him taxes on their allowance."

BUT GOD'S LOVE LETTERS ARE A REMINDER TO ME THAT...

Ye have seen what I did unto the Egyptians, and *how* I bare you on eagles' wings, and brought you unto myself.

-- Exodus 19:4

I'VE HEARD IT SAID ABOUT ME THAT...

"That dude seriously freaks me out. His skin is so pale that whenever it snows, people think he's shedding."

BUT GOD'S LOVE LETTERS ARE A REMINDER TO ME THAT…

Ye are the light of the world.

-- Matthew 5:14

I'VE HEARD IT SAID ABOUT ME THAT...

"His in-laws proclaimed him so worthless that when he and his wife sadly considered divorcing each other, her parents offered to pay for the promise rings."

BUT GOD'S LOVE LETTERS ARE A REMINDER TO ME THAT...

The Lord hath appeared of old unto me, *saying*, Yea, I have loved thee with an everlasting love: therefore with loving-kindness have I drawn thee.

-- Jeremiah 31:3

I'VE HEARD IT SAID ABOUT ME THAT…

"He's so boring that when he began walking on water while being baptized, the pastor took a moment to text his lunch order."

BUT GOD'S LOVE LETTERS ARE A REMINDER TO ME THAT...

But as many as received him, to them gave he power to become the sons of God, *even* to them that believe on his name:

-- John 1:12

I'VE HEARD IT SAID ABOUT ME THAT...

"Several of my housekeepers mentioned Dizzney's lower-class home being so unbelievably tiny that in order to prevent further ceiling damage, he has to stop raising the toilet lid."

BUT GOD'S LOVE LETTERS ARE A REMINDER TO ME THAT...

Surely goodness and mercy shall follow me all the days of my life: and I will dwell in the house of the Lord for ever.

-- Psalm 23:6

I'VE HEARD IT SAID ABOUT ME THAT...

*"Talk about low to the ground! That inch-high hobbit is so short that when his first baby was born, **it** held **him**."*

BUT GOD'S LOVE LETTERS ARE A REMINDER TO ME THAT...

For in him we live, and move, and have our being; as certain also of your own poets have said, For we are also his offspring.

-- Acts 17:28

I'VE HEARD IT SAID ABOUT ME THAT...

"You should avoid ever shaking hands with him at all costs! His palms are so unnaturally sweaty, his adult diapers come with matching gloves."

BUT GOD'S LOVE LETTERS ARE A REMINDER TO ME TO...

Call unto me, and I will answer thee, and show thee great and mighty things, which thou knowest not.

-- Jeremiah 33:3

I'VE HEARD IT SAID ABOUT ME THAT...

"His sense of direction is so bad, his prayers get answered by coal miners."

BUT GOD'S LOVE LETTERS ARE A REMINDER TO ME THAT...

How precious also are thy thoughts unto me, O God! how great is the sum of them!

-- Psalm 139:17

I'VE HEARD IT SAID ABOUT ME THAT...

"That Dizzney guy once prepared dinner for some of his neighbors, and all I can say is...last month when a group of thieving arsonists targeted his home, several fire-fighters sacrificed their very lives just to put out every deadly blaze in the poor guy's house - right after they added more fuel to the one in the kitchen."

BUT GOD'S LOVE LETTERS ARE A REMINDER TO ME THAT...

BEHOLD, WHAT manner of love the Father hath bestowed upon us, that we should be called the sons of God: therefore the world knoweth us not, because it knew him not.

-- 1 John 3:1

I'VE HEARD IT SAID ABOUT ME THAT...

"He should be banned from having a gym membership here. That Hulk-wannabe is so frail that at our annual athlete's luncheon, he broke his neck swallowing."

BUT GOD'S LOVE LETTERS ARE A REMINDER TO ME THAT...

The LORD thy God in the midst of thee *is* mighty; he will save, he will rejoice over thee with joy; he will rest in his love, he will joy over thee with singing.

-- Zephaniah 3:17

I'VE HEARD IT SAID ABOUT ME THAT...

"He could never get a date with a glamorous babe. The only woman who ever loved him worshipfully was a hay-slumbering farm-girl who was such a homely bumpkin, a pig woke up next to her one morning and swore off late-night slopping."

BUT GOD'S LOVE LETTERS ARE A REMINDER TO ME THAT...

Thine eyes did see my substance, yet being unperfect; and in thy book all *my members* were written, *which* in continuance were fashioned, when *as yet there was* none of them.

-- Psalm 139:16

AND LASTLY, I'VE HEARD IT SAID ABOUT ME THAT...

"I don't have any exaggerated criticisms to make about Dizzney because he really is a good man! I broke my leg yesterday morning and just can't get around – but because his ears are so long, I'm praying he'll let me use them as crutches."

BUT GOD'S LOVE LETTERS ARE THE PERFECT REMINDER TO ME THAT...

In whom also we have obtained an inheritance, being predestinated according to the purpose of him who worketh all things after the counsel of his own will:

That we should be to the praise of his glory, who first trusted in Christ.

-- Ephesians 1:11-12

NOW I DON'T KNOW ABOUT YOU, BUT THE NEXT TIME THIS CHILD OF GOD BEGINS FEELING INSECURE AND WORTHLESS DUE TO OVERBEARING FEELINGS OF INADEQUACY CREEPING IN - OR I GET WIND OF OTHERS MERCILESSLY SPOTLIGHTING FLAWS OF MINE SUCH AS THIS...

"His sense of movement is so underdeveloped that when he was a baby, he crawled with a cane."

...I, FAULT DIZZNEY, WILL QUOTE TO MYSELF COMPASSION-SCENTED, VICTORY-SOAKED PASSAGES FROM SOME OF GOD'S LOVE LETTERS TO ME, SUCH AS...

What shall we then say to these things? If God *be* for us, who *can be* against us?

Romans 8:31

Bless them which persecute you: bless, and curse not.

Romans 12:14

SO BASK CONFIDENTLY IN GOD'S LOVE LETTERS TO YOU, LOVE THOSE CRITICAL NEIGHBORS ANYWAY...AND STRIVE TO ALLOW EVEN A WEARY SPIRIT TO LAUGH JOYOUSLY THROUGH LIFE – OR YOU'LL FIND YOURSELF SPINNING NAUSEOUSLY AROUND DIZZILYLAND!!!

All scriptures taken from the King James Version of the Holy Bible

THIS PUBLICATION IS DEDICATED TO THE LOVING MEMORY OF MICHELLE FLANDERS, WHO HAS GONE ON TO EXPERIENCE THE INDESCRIBABLE JOY THAT ONLY COMES WITH WALKING SIDE-BY-SIDE WITH OUR LORD AND SAVIOR, CHRIST JESUS. MAN, HOW SHE LOVED TO LAUGH – JUST LIKE ME!!!

REPENtERTAINMENT COMING FROM

THURD/WIRM MEDIA EUGENICS

STAFF BIOGRAPHIES

(Great...now our creditors can track us)

DONNELL OWENS - Chicago-born Christian author/ comedian & movie lover, currently residing near Los Angeles. A complicated individual, Mr. Owens is a man whose reflection thinks they should see other people.

BABY CHRISTIAN - the questionably insane alter-ego of author Donnell Owens, who performs Christian comedy under this stage name for his own protection (from a terrorist agency of physically abused, bedside alarm clocks). Baby Christian has a ton of experience appearing in front of excited audiences, mostly for police-station line-ups. His motto: IF I FAIL TO MAKE YOU LAUGH, CONSIDER THE PRICE OF ADMISSION A CASH ADVANCE AGAINST MY NEXT UNEMPLOYMENT CHECK.

Caron R. Harts - Web Master, E-Commerce Manager & Web Marketing Manager, THURD/WIRM MEDIA EUGENICS

www.thurd-wirm.com

DON'T FORGET TO SAY HELLO TO US!!!

THURD/WIRM MEDIA EUGENICS **is a publishing and entertainment company specializing in Christian humor. Peek in on us at *www.thurd-wirm.com*. You can facebook us at THURD WIRM, follow us on Twitter and check us out on YouTube. You can also contact us at 818-288-2901. You can order our books through us in hardback/ softback and e-book formats. And looky, you can book our on-staff Christian comedian BABY CHRISTIAN to perform at your church-related events. *WARNING!!!* That guy is so out there, his multiple personalities are soliciting donations so he can see a shrink. TO GOD BE ALL THE GLORY!!! IT'S IN JESUS' PRECIOUS NAME WE PRAY!!!!**

BLESSINGS!!!!! LAUGHTER!!!!!! CHRIST JESUS!!!!! MERRY HEARTS!!!!!